NAME

1 Real Time

Someone's reading Russian poetry, has a volume in her hand answering a knock at the door, You can forget that accent, fella, we're pretty low-budget... returning the leather-bound book to it's place in the shelves.

He sets his case and some brooms by the door, drops a fart, being himself, You wouldn't believe... as he speaks she remembers a cast of unfortunates ending-up at this door ..how many fuckin' doors I've knocked on... she trips the deadlock, kills the front lights and pours him a drink wondering how profanity comes across in sign.

He doesn't seem to like anything or know anybody nice, puts-on accents to amuse himself with the suckers, *Mwahaha*... chuckling into her glass parallel with his worthless charm she can pretend to know what he's talking about. Her murderous thoughts are shaken by a dart through his neck, I step from the shadows nursing the antique crossbow, This guy's annoying from upstairs... he's squirming on the floor suppressing a ruptured artery. Darling... she's trying it on, I don't know what to say, she sounds about ten, We have to move, darling, it's all changing... she says it again, I can't help smiling, blood all over my face *hwWAA*... my breath escapes with ecstatic fury, she joins me on the floor, her eyes huge, irises blank *HHAaa*... a bloody kiss over the twitching corpse.

A nerd's doing science, loves that stuff, tedious yet captivating like an inept robbery in progress, the book expands on a poorly phrased law of thermodynamics fumbling at natures bra-strap *..it's all about entropy, the skirmish-line of temporal existence...*

Someone walks in unexpectedly, surprise evident Where's the car-park.. The new Ducati.. Where am I... he checks behind the door before heading down the stairs, an unusual weapon slung at his back.

A young courier's coming up plotting to open his palm and raise his eye-brows, he's been practising the move, THIS time... thinking out very loud on the quiet stairs. He hears the priming of an unfamiliar weapon, they're probably anxious for the parcel and they sound nervous.. he picks-up his pace, the other guy fires defensively, two.. three.. four.. down into the stairwell, it's a grenade launcher, five.. six..

Flats above the rubble are open to the selfish lonely street like a noir movie set, there'll be access problems now even without doors.. power and water issues, they'll have to discuss the rent and the nerd has class tomorrow, leave by the window and scramble to the ground.. he's hoping there's something clean.

Pacing a cluttered room a lanky middle-aged psychopath studies a messy hand- written page, scratches absently at his crotch *Yes... resonant but colourless and bland, inviting announcement or enquiry without cadence or inflection...* the full-stop's been turned into a comma with *sans prelude...* in a little girls hand and a different pen.

The scrappy journal continues at a fresh paragraph *..A neutral syllable with a greeting coining the vernacular...* the girls tiny script has managed to fit *appropriate* above *vernacular* dotted with a little flower, the killer seems agitated reviewing the absurd ledger, That's a plan, of course it'll work... gerund verb, duct-tape, and a knife.

Another old psycho... I think he's a rello, backstory for that girl... Ah, thanks... drops her head back, plaster figures pour nothing from urns around the large domed ceiling, she stifles a yawn bracing against the oppressive continuity, I'm just going for cigarettes, darling...

Trembling with eternal bliss and trying to light a cigarette when she recognises Yes... a bland resonance with no trace of bias then Hi... smooth as a slug, she knows what she's hearing the surprise is how well it works, the target drawn automatically into the shadows. That maniac was in the lane... Hmm...

That skinny old guy, Yairss.. Yeahz... cradled in the speeding taxi practising the resonant tone, city lights reflected fleeting across the car, rosemary soft in her hair and I breathe into it I'm starving... Yurzs... she sees my hunger and raises her stiletto, a couple of cherubs are following the taxi, the guy's their case-study.

A red glow deep in the ground exposes heavy veins haemorrhaging into the street, there's a cruel incessant wail and the sound of teeth gnashing, the angels look for meaning and find mocking laughter through dank timber stalls with babies screaming nailed to the crude planks, Hope they're not load-bearing... the joke wasted on hags without eyes lurking on a misty river-bank, Stygian women, he gazes into the crystal ball, Hi, nice seein' me... wink and point, the horror never ends.

They take some sort of bridge, throw rocks at the souls on the ferry, and arrive at egocentric bubbles, times and places swelling with inspiration and fragmenting in a temporal fountain, Hey, we're back here... a kitchen with a kid burning toast. Yeah, we came right through, that's the taxi-driver... there's countless angels studying what otherwise just is.

..semi-independent through the apex, linear but tangential... a substitute teacher continues the mid-term lesson describing a perspective she doesn't share, No, we'll look at specific colour in Causality... well versed in the standard model, just never actually done it.

2 Graveyard shift at the observatory, the girl from the bus-stop studies the cool spectrum analysis What's the spike there... Hydrogen, it's nearly all hydrogen. We're gettin' a better collector... What are you looking for... the junior astronomer's been watching this girl, catches the same bus, It's the deep-space-field, way out there, it's back in time... Time... Yeah, that's billions of years ago... he explains expansion, she flounders, So all this was over there.. thinks Wave to yourself.. and realises her mistake, you'd have to wave long ago.

Three a.m. and they've found champagne at the bottom of the little fridge, What's it all mean, Finkelstein.. HA... I think it's rhetorical but Finkelstein was studying exactly this when his flat was destroyed demonstrating the point, takes a moment to pass the heavy bottle, It's all about entropy... touching his lips like it's a secret.

UHg, you know, all that poverty and hate... she hoists the expensive magnum for a two-handed swig, They live on garbage dumps...

pointing at him out of focus, dribbling, wipes her mouth on her knee ..In slums made of crap... drops her hand emphatically, he's trying to make a cogent response, I doubt he'll get laid.

A dark symphony, rich colours running into each other, deep strong punchlines reaching out, no-one shares their perspective, the moment fragments like alien fruit maturing. *..the fresh position of the advancing wave-front equals the sum of inspiration in the previous position of the wave...* Yes, its wave-length.. No, it's arbitrary.. please.. the telescope is all through here.. that guy's over there.. he's old... angels are drifting off but this one's still not clear on the principles of sequencing, she instructs him on the unfolding events The decimating stitch-in-time effect... he doesn't say anything hovering there watching the fountain.

In the big telescope old Finkelstein can just make something out, way at the back of space, Looks like some sort of logo, put it on the plasma... the screen's black with a small grey smudge. Is that h.d... a much sharper smudge, more like a scratch, Bring it up and we'll run the filters... heavily pixelated six months later it's still too blurry and after a full year collecting and collating they take a consensus, *Happy Birthday...* the primeval greeting's apparent, Finkelstein didn't want to say it, We can't publish this… he has to make certain of that.

Geodetically past the north-pole Putin posters are prevalent promoting some fracas or another, two submariners have been loose in Murmansk and feel they'll get lucky with these rich-chicks, spilling out of the bar intent to score at slightly crossed purpose How old are you... it's a compliment, she quotes poetry at him, they hear a scuffle and know what it is, he makes his move.. cold moonlight glints in the tiny razor and his life gushes from behind his jaw, he seems surprised, she pulls him closer Darling, it's all lies... maybe a comment on the sentimental poetry, can only be helpful and sounds great whispered in Russian. She's passionately kissing the wound, the sucked-out heart persists with sporadic noncommittal contractions.. but much prettier written in Cyrillic.

Mounted ranks form-up in waves of hysteria building until the lines break and the spirited Arabian horses bolt in every direction, we need a new strategy, Tunnel extensively and occupy a subterranean country... Get lots of really big balloons... Take the heads off matches... everyone goes quiet. These amateur zealots have been doomed for some time, pyp... (nineteen.. eighteen..) a drone counts down beeping with a heavy accent every five seconds (seventeen.. sixteen..) pyp… here comes an attack helicopter.. we all hear it.. pyp.. (nine.. eight..).. Goodbye habibi... the villagers scatter with racehorse enthusiasm (seven.. six..) pyp.. pyp.. pyp..

Time's like putty to the aliens, they're pretty smug wormholing around looking for signs of inspiration, closing the file on this carnal species, a behavioural study to do and they're watching the news, Let me get this straight… but it makes no sense. She speeds-up the TV feed and dubs-in something with banjos, the aliens are rolling on the floor and it's not that funny, nitrous-oxide's accumulating in the thin ammonia atmosphere, they might crash, time slipping from their grasp.. Just gimme a minute... she doesn't have a minute, BRACE…

A chip's been wetwired into someones brain and without calibration he can't read a brochure on *The Many Benefits of Cyber Enhancement*. The Doc has worse things to worry about, that catastrophe may go badly and these quiet corridors burst with emergency, he quits work early to worry at home, all night if needed.. drinking alone in bloody scrubs under a dim naked light.

Still high on pain-killers that guy hopes to somehow take control of the chip, he won't try lighting another cigarette, planning a casual introduction that might include Could you light this, please... Hey, scooby-doob... this big guy seems delighted accepting the challenge. It's only a poorly rolled cigarette but his friends perk-up, the waitress steps in and I just watch as the guy with the bandages and malamute eyes pulls a Thai cigar from his sock, it gets around like an Olympic torch.

Someone's reading to him something funny, everybody's talking going anywhere but here and against public opinion that waitress has elected to drive north with me.

 Should be there in about eighteen hours... Long as nothin' bad happens… into six lanes of headlights and a northerly sunrise, it's almost noon, cold with a warm breeze, the sky's thick and seems to keep swelling, no-one's ever seen anything like it but it looks like those oil fires, Yeah, Jarhead... Desert Storm, yeah… it's nothing like it, probably Yellowstone, there's rumours, strange radar images..

This abandoned hotel has ninety-three floors with stairs to the penthouse, there's loads of alcohol, she's at the full-length windows looking at history while I mix drinks. A giant crater dips along the ocean side where tsunamis take dirt.. here's one now.. random jets of flame erupt from the ground venting toxic gas from deep in the rocks. Highway-lights cross the burning desert over a ribbon of cars grinding awkwardly south, there could be dogs barking you can't tell from up here. Sea-water swamps the western rim releasing a cloud bigger than a small country lit orange and pink with lava spitting at it, a nervous laugh as the building takes the sonic blast, I need a drink... Yeah, thanks... she wipes her lip handing me the glass, wild lightening back there, rolling thunder and sharp acid rain.

We soon reach the crater, fumes pouring over the edge like a big experiment, she drops-back gears with clutch-shuffling talent and the raging v-eight ignites cresting in the volatile fog, a fireball launched into a frozen moment, Who are all these people, and what's so funny…

Hey, did I fall asleep... a woman's up on one arm, Coffee... this guy's already up, twenty-dollars richer under a secret new contract. Late afternoon and still in bed, crystals dusting the little mirror on the tray among the ruins of monumental joints *BANG*, not high powered, kids next door shooting at the wildlife *BANGBANG, BANG*, they might've found BANG a nest, NOoo… holding her limp body, smoothing her hair, a single shot has pierced the back of her lovely head, the small hole belies extensive damage. Sign here, and here... a baby cries, it's a hot summer night, a body-bag's wheeled slowly away and he mutters esoterically Twenty lousy bucks…

I can probably get you a satch... I'm only gone about an hour and there's a party, maybe a riot, I barely make it inside, It's those lipstick vampires... Where... Hi... she's upstairs with a purple drink, her friend's huffing a Moroccan trumpet and hands it off, Damned villagers...

SMASH... they're at the windows, Don'worry'boudit... delicious blonde hash, I hear sirens, YOU GUYS TAKE THE CAR… dull on the empty stairs, Here... over the balcony and across the neighbours roof, TAXI.. airport thanks… and leave these lights behind, they want to be in Romania to forge some kind of nexus. Carpathian Mountains, Transylvania, a storm drawing in, there's the castle along that cliff-edged goat-track, the driver keeps passing out and the horses might be trying to escape. It's dark and raining so a description wouldn't do justice, gargoyles and parapets invisible in the gloom, flying buttresses holding something against the cliff.. something alive.. a granite hall.. an oversized cauldron sits alone in the dusty barren space, torches fighting darkness all around and upstairs a sound of black rags flapping, I'm speechless, it all seems stolen. The giant doors have finally closed against the wolves and a fire's raging under the conspicuous big pot, I hear whispering but no-one's there. The vampires start singing, I still don't say anything and a shiny blue vortex makes a surprising appearance in the glowing hot crucible, JUMP IN...

3 Requ*s% im*&^iate exTr$tion... the scramblers on the fritz.

Sold himself out for twenty-bucks and some intrigue, eeuAGH... the diphthong of death, they all scream like that, Bloody ninjas... the reference falls from his seasoned lips, the miles starting to show, I've seen stuff.. in Calcutta... he's gotta get outta here.. candid and loose with this stranger, says she's a dancer, she has those genes and wants to help.

Catalonia, he can't leave her alone, Do you mind... she fixes her ponytail, Dos whiskies, porfavor… it's all wrong, he may be hiding something, the bar heats-up and he steps down an alley looking back all the way to the airport, it can't be easy.

In Sydney.. there's a five-minute Delacroix in a line-up at the museum, in custody with a crowd of well-heeled strangers and a numeric soap-opera progressing through pointless algorithms, he's soon at the beach, upstairs with scotch and milk when those women walk in, there's blood on her shoe, it's almost noon. Darling... she doesn't touch him, they move to the balcony and he's there on a hollow premise You're just in time... she goes Yuess... resonant and blank, knows what she's talking about, the fresh ocean breeze is powerless against her and the other-one's dress waves by choice slowly and darkly backwards. Authentic art anecdotes, Modigliani seems an alright kid, and over drinks he'll agree to anything.. they'll walk along the beach.

The ocean's stopped, seagulls won't land on it, there's no shadows or apparent light-source and the colour's dropping out, the sky looks different and now the birds are frozen, they're in a black & white photo, How are you doing this... Doing what... it sounds tweaked, an alien laugh, Darling, are you alright... that laugh, and her lips moving counter to the words.

Marauders are hard at work reducing organic matter to send through a generated spatial vortex, G.S.V, to some distant galaxy they say and I don't see why they'd lie, must be a big operation.. planets.. stars.. God, if I had that job... What... God's finished dinner and He's looking for a diversion, Oh, it's just this guy... a few gopis skim the misplaced file, it's archival, not archangel, Some guy you say… Mmm, Garry-something. Wants to be a problem across half a universe... Ambitious, how about a planet-killer dark-matter ray... Yeah, no thanks.. he'd really like a job with these pirates… the gopis giggle, God pretends he doesn't get it. Garry's dying breaths hurt, the carbon scouts are almost too busy to notice a tiny corpse decaying rapidly in the deep hydrochloric pressure, Yecch.. what's that... this insecure alien's still very new, everyone's sick of it. Another guy's waving tendrils sampling the heavy acid air Smells toxic… leering at the timid marauder but it must have been something and they'd better take a look, How'd it get in here... Someone's got bugs… the rookies new name.

4 We've gotta do something about these damn aliens... an infectious sense of purpose and there's talk of conspiracy.. we might be terrorists. I don't know anyone so it's a surprise being chosen for a suicide mission, Pilot this big-arse nuke into radio waves around an invisible spaceship... Buy me a drink and we'll talk... he zeros-in on some microwaves in space and silently rams the invisible aliens before the eerie hush of a multi-megaton blast.

Standard deviates relax in long low waves of normalcy for maybe a year when little lights swarm above the mountains, a kid ditches her cigarette and jumps down from the window They're comin' outta that big blue one... she fidgets and runs to tell her brother leaving the old army buddies to deal with the alien menace stretching along the horizon. The crescent of lights is a cross-section, an umbrella of weird objects swiftly covering this sector CRASH... a small rock-shaped hole appears in the roof, a heavy ferro-carbon fragment that looks like wet glass pitches into the night sky, souvenir of a previous encounter.

Technicians have pieced together enough of the ill-fated scout vessel to have a good idea what happened, *spec req :)) \\ hpps: # eradication :((\ toxic species &% hzmat @ //blahblahwhereverthehell-this-is, asap, thanks...* Hey, wanna watch... That's so greeb... the young pilots are embarrassed for the guy, no-one's watching as semi- autonomous satellites appear in a G.S.V. and prepare to vitrify the wrong small world.

Yes I draw a stipend from the state right now but I'll be an artist if I get this grant... the logic's sound and it's a sizeable endorsement, Lyudmyla's happy until drugs and hopeless causes see her cold and hardened on the streets of Smolensk, turning-out nudes for a few lousy roubles, portraits of pets, landscapes, anything to stay high producing astute civic murals alone by the train tracks, NASDROVYA LYUDMYLA, dosvidanya... Yuri finally talks about his fearless little sister, we can't stand-up but everyone raises their glass NASDROVYA, tovarich...

Great food aboard a Russian submarine if you like this sort of stuff, good vodka and women in the crew, comfortable until someone runs a test. It escalates from a very bad start, the results consigned directly to the water along with all souls and a brief radio signal, a few lines that may change the world, the reason they've taken this desperate mission, ones and zeros encrypted under the ice with zeros and ones, it could be a code, only one person can make sense of this.

Wait, I'll get my big furry hat... eventually wake the professor to let them in and they'll do the data, DOCtor MATalov... loud to mask how wrecked they are and that they've brought women.

People are knocking things over, the old professor fires-up the computer, Here, 'Toli.. ANATOLI.. oh, hello miss... she smiles, 'Toli rubs his chin scouring the binary message 'Zdigital, yudjurztnidxawftviyr... they download a free bundle and make a hard-copy for the boss, Happy Birthday... it's in all the papers.

..the primordial cosmic artefact finally brought to light at the cost of so many lives. Dr. Finkelstein, suspect in the disappearance of two junior techs, is now a person of interest over a string of cold-case homicides spanning half a century in a macabre twist to an astronomical cover-up...

That girl... alone in his cell Finkelstein has plenty of time to think, mostly about that girl, Her hair... he's fixated, growing old in the criminal obsession, cruising bus-stops abducting so many lovely young women, sobbing to himself when Criminal Justice steps in, he knows a guy in forensics, this won't be cheap. Dr. Finkelstein's up for a Nobel prize with no-one left to share it, just a few guys in the forensics lab and this crooked public attorney, it'll mean a sweet payday for him, a new life, something on the Continent, but it's a solitary tux laid out and Finkelstein takes the time to shower and shave covered in spatter from the early-morning slaughter.

A heavy weight sits on his chest, his arm hurts and his whole left side collapses in the mirror, that girl's nursing him on the bathroom floor, he's twisting to see her his arm growing painfully useless, if he can.. just.. twist..

Washing hangs over a torrent of life coursing with sweaty circadian rhythm, fresh donkey-shit is quickly tracked-out along the road with small birds darting in at it, the sunset stolen by highway-lights polarising the masses with the shallow horizon, TRES BONITAS... it's those guys from the overpass and this is someones attractive cousin and her friends, they ignore them and stroll among the tourists along the bright noisy strip, Ola.. espresso porfavor, y tequila.. gracias Rosa… someplace people tell lies about.

The heat, the well-cut clothes and the smell of cigars, coffee and great food validate the loud music and coloured lights strung across the lane. Feral dogs sniff along the kerb flanking a fresh wave of urchins as a suave bunch of guys in loose suits climb into original 'fifties American cars, Isn't that your cousin... Yeah.. HOOLY... he's coming over side-stepping taxis, Looking good bae...

He pinches the lapel, touches his hat, Muchachittas... embracing his vivacious cousin he finishes her drink, We're going to Francesca's party, jous should come... gold pin, a Russian cigarette, his friend's wearing sunglasses at night and talking to Carmen and Gabriela, it's as good as it gets.. time and place.. you at the centre.. THE END.

I'm goin' for a smoke Hey, is that a flying-saucer... an empty space hangs in the air some meters above the backyard, it scans with an imperceptible beam and the strange invisible craft might have already left. I can see over the fence, across the road and past the mountains to the city and the ocean and take the trippy experience for granted, sitting here smoking looking along the coast to a curved horizon. It's snowing glitter, I close my eyes but the glitter persists sparkling against a metallic field, lights flashing in titanium panels swimming into focus with dozens of me kneeling, stumbling and vomiting in a shallow milky pool. I'm stunned, a gestalt, I've read about this, we're all me, stunned, belching the thin white fluid. Finally open my eyes.. hurl.. alone and central with an altered sense of scale, stepping out of the shallow pool into a standard honeycomb cell and growing a heavy ferro-organic chrysalis to launch alienated across space with time-bending speed.. nothin' to it.

Oo oowa-aa-aa… a very early young woman can hardly contain herself staining her nails red, Uggh… mum's not impressed, she'll show her friends. ARGH ARGH.. Oo-Oo-Oo… back-flips on the primitive furniture, this is significant. The matriarch ambles across to smell the future in her granddaughters hair as a ghostly cold light sweeps through the cave, something semi-organic falls from the sky in a plasma of troubled entropy crashing not far away, Hi… the artificial guy doesn't know what he's talking about, he's delirious.

5 Greater Mumton

Look, Millie, a giraffe… Emily squeezes her mother's fingers, Franklin pushes his face into dad's overcoat .. And clowns… they squeeze tighter and bury deeper shaking their little head, mum forces a smile, dad looks away. Darkness creeps through the town finding the children peeking over the edge of their blankets, wardrobes filled with malice, cold terror under every bed, a distant background of circus music and that's only the beginning. The kids hear distraught voices late at night We have to buy tickets... But dear... the volume drops, We could hide... and in a whisper Go to the caves...

Gangs roam the streets in tiny cars, clowns tumble out and stare blankly squirting obscenely from artificial flowers. The teacher glances back spying yellow fuzzy hair and big red noses through the bushes, balloons bobbing above, oversized shoes protruding and chilling calls of toy horns and slide whistles, Everyone in two neat lines.. hold your partners hand... herding children into a bus. Even the most secret caves are filled with refugees and kids, We'll go north.. start a new life... dad spits to confirm the promise, demonstrating commitment and faith but mum's not buying it, can't go on the roads or through the musty swamp, they'll have to stick to the ridges.

Emily's shoes hurt and Franklin's trying to keep-up in those big sandals, the little trooper, and mum's had about enough CAN WE STOP... her voice lost in the dense undergrowth, dad's a long way up the ridge.. swears he'll come back for them.

She meets someone, they open a store on the mountain, home-school Millie and Frank and a dozen other kids with their fed-up mothers and together build a school and a town-hall and look into the appropriate council by-laws, We're a mining town.. Mumton... the women still think it's funny but these future kids don't see the joke, busy with jobs and cars.. on roads.

What happened to those doobs... Right here... granny-dance onto the patio. The old ladies clink glasses celebrating fresh degrees of frailty and surprise glimpses in mirrors and don't stop talking 'til they've eaten all the cakes.

Those where the days, just ol' auntie Alice... No, she's gone... So what'll we do... I'm getting married… Yeah, I mean about the town... Yeah, the guy at the bookstore… meeting adjourned marvelling at the diamond ring.

Trouble at the swamp, something's taken someone's arm... Call an ambulance, and find-out whose arm... Emily sets herself a large whisky, these are her problems. Chain of command, logistics, a team but the top remains vulnerable and they never cry. So lonely, self-pity welling in her eyes, a second glass fermenting her thoughts, You don't see many women Generals... she doesn't care, her mind's taken by the uniform, way too small with leather gloves and a riding crop, Hell yeah, I'm doin' it… she's only a mayor so I doubt she can but it's her town, freehold, she could sell it. They each take a nice cut, prudently keep a dividend on future gross and establish trusts.

Oh wow... she doesn't say it, learnt to stay cool squandering money, better say something How fast does it go... the guy's stuck with how fast this monster might go, coupla-thousand tonne, four masts, jib sticking out, it's probably a real slug, There's another bar in the focsle with a sundeck on top, the aft sundeck has a transparent freshwater pool sunk into the bistro and there's a moon-pool in the lounge under the auditorium, it lights-up, you gotta see that. It takes a crew of eight with another dozen ancillary but that's okay, this beauty's all about accommodation.. check it out, huge underwater windows.. and watch this..

They skirt the coast a few months before heading out for the sunny South Seas, develop a flow with the bar staff selecting destinations by enthusiasm, backpackers love it, live music.. some people go ashore to buy Harleys and tour the countryside.

6 ..six tanks, twelve fifty-cal. A.P.C.s and two attack-helicopters, ordnance for a full- scale assault plus a full company, Ma'am... Thank you Sergeant, secure the perimeter, get intel, you know the drill… she

slaps the riding-crop down, unties her blouse and loosens the button on the tight little shorts, ahh... feet up with a large single-malt.

On her second glass, carefully relighting a cigar, What is it, soldier... the guy fidgets with his hat, You might want to see this, General... she brings her drink to look on a horde of frightened villagers, Feed 'em and find somewhere for 'em to stay.. and get someone that knows the language…

The General calls her tank Portia after the tiny spider and people think it's sarcasm, so lonely, jodhpurs, aviators, shark-skin gloves, she makes the twirly-sign and we advance as a front through the jungle, choppers standing-by and A.P.C.s with infantry mopping-up Taking fire, Sarge... We've got movement, General.. grid echo niner.. request airstrike... *kchhh..* Copy... multitasking the strike, keeping the line and targeting an installation in joint with the stoner crew, bunch of weirdos, In position, Ma'am... objective secure.. *tchhht..* Got something to the west, General... *kchh..* Copy that... airstrike into the tropical sunset.

Back at the secure beach-head the troops catch some last rays before retiring to mess, a party went out on A.T.V.s and haven't returned, We can't just sit here... Get a grip, Private, could be anything out there, I wouldn't like to speculate.. werewolves probably, and zombies.. who knows, maybe even vampires...

Starving vampires, skinny elbows and knees massed over the writhing victims, they push the quad bikes into view hoping someone comes to get them, Not me... Pussy, who's comin' to check it out...

They've been gone a while, I don't hear the bikes... C'mon, we all know what's happened, something got 'em... HEY... a survivor slams the door, he's leaning on it to brace it with his back but he's exhausted, Vampires got us... Told ya'... WATER... he crashes to his knees in the bloody shreds of a uniform and pours the bottle over his face, distinctive twin puncture wounds cover his body, we have to shoot him before he turns, Acceptable losses.. desirable outcomes.. objectives.. shit, we need a plan.. wish the General was here...

She's at the other side of the island digesting alcohol sorting personal issues, So who is she, Gunny, what's that accent... Yeah, that accent. I walk into the C.O.s and there she is, reckons it's an alternate reality...

The General rolls back onto the beach for extraction, Don't give me that malarkey, get the damn bikes... she could go rounds with a pillow but deploys into the dunes, guns guns guns in the gentle calm before dawn, artillery, napalm strikes and fifty-cal. wooden stakes, full maple jacket. The assault seems more protracted than it is ..*kchh* Say-again ..*tchht*.. Roger that.. Stand-down air-support and assemble on the beach for debrief...

..and when not actively sleeping I'll be unavailable.. are we clear, Sergeant... Good-night, General, extro in ten days... that's eight days ago, someone should do something.. there's no answer.. they venture inside. Cobwebs and tattered curtains, mattress folded on the rusty bed, an old picture caked with time, it leaves a bright spot on the wall, I think it's the General.. *pwhoo*.. with this guy, signed with a marker, No crayons, buddy?.. Hey yeah, she's out of uniform... they pan over the empty quarters, just an old photo from a different future and a sock, it's hard to make-out. So who signed these orders, that's a mayoral seal, and have a go at the date... Y'know, I heard something once... That's how rumours start, Kowalski, this has to be a structural thing, I've often thought this might be an alternate reality... So she's here but in some other dimension... It depends what you mean by she, or here, or dimension, but sure, I suppose so... Wonder what she's doing now... I see her in a Nazi-uniform.. Gestapo hat and a leather balconette... Yeah but you're sick, she's most likely a nun.. suspender-belt and high-heels... A slutty cop, or a nurse... Where's the damn General, we ship-out in two days...

7 Isn't that your mother... an elderly couple in jeans and carrying helmets, Hello Archie... Yeah, hi mum, it's just Arch now... Hello son, how's things... Fine... That's great, you look good... dad fist-bumps the air. This deteriorates, his friends stream it, they gather like nothing happened and race drift-cars home to places we can't afford, reconditioned showrooms and health-spas. Archer's done-out a Leagues Club and pulls-up to automatic lighting, directional audio and

a virtual cityscape, something's over there.. make a fist and the room fills with holographic A.I s having a great time drinking cold Coopers beer. He wanders through Car Accs, doubletaps something, Kat... Hi Arch... she presses him up, What's up... Nuthin'.. saw a nice beer ad... I love those... she raises a finger and swipes right, neon streets take the wall, nothing stands out, It'll be a loop... this might be it, make a fist.. it's a movie, Oh yeah, I've seen the book...

Some time later he drives out and finds her in the renovated factory, they helicopter to the coast and take the ocean cruiser up to the brand new beach-house.. just the basement so far but solid and self contained, secure underwater in the tide, they're soon in each others arms slurring devotion in deep filtered light. Family life suits them, dropping off progeny with wads of money and names like antibiotics, I think she makes them up, Call 'em both Moe.. *Wa'ssup, Moe...* We should move...

He lets himself into Kate's new place, she's mixing a drink, there's a hologram of a piano, he sits in with a sweet joint, Don't give-up... What's that supposed to mean... You look serious... Piss-off... smoking in heavy silence, Nina Simone hammering the grand piano whispering deep injustice, I'm pregnant... Wow Kat, how far along, little Moe... he goes to touch her belly, she knocks his hand away and walks outside, backless dress and bare feet catching the light, I wanna have it over there...

Arch pours the shaker and notices the hacked-up fruit, Have it over there... like it's his idea, behind her, arm around her against heavy industrial silhouettes and solid traffic, signs coming on and birds going home over a messy sunset, she takes the fat roach and turns, I'm not calling it Moe...

They meet an undignified end on the way, all that arrives is bad news and a respectable legacy, little Alcyone and Dionysus are proud to print their name in coloured pencil on forms with Kathi and Arch's people, no real change for the fresh orphans but it's a strange day, one that sticks in their mind. The kids are teenage when they locate a grandmother living on a yacht and a few weeks later they join Nanna languishing in the tropical South Pacific, their mothers mother Emily, People call me Millie.. Ali and Dan isn't it.. Katherine's kids...

Ali keeps a low profile showing around noon in the downstairs lounge huffing spliff and sipping Baileys by the moon-pool. Dan's writing poetry for a girl from the islands, she's taken-up watercolour amusing the geriatrics who poke at them inappropriately, he points-out they're a bunch of dicks and takes Nge'k away, he rescues her Oh, Nyack... mangling the name, kissing franticly, they look the type to kill themselves.

The Mate sets the jib coming-about leeward of an atoll, hair gathered from all over the ship is secreted in the folds of the sail and rains out over Nanna and her friends. Turning off a fridge is one thing but pouring out all that vodka and replacing it with sea-water is personal, Hey Dan, someone's left you this atoll.. you just have to stay the night...

Twelve-meter sloop Cameron two days out of Broome in for a squall, We'll be okay... Hercules lowering the sail, Adonis at the helm, Dan and Nge'k hanging-on at the bow riding the rough sea. Yous better get below... he's wrestling the heavy sheet, they squeeze past into the clean minimalist cabin, hatches battened, Do you guys like spaghetti.. ew, there's sugar in everything... the kids stare out the porthole, jettisoned at the first inhabited spot. No wi-fi, a few huts, fish-dinner and an outrigger by starlight to some other island.. Dan pisses on the firewood.

Civilisation at last.. myspace, Where's Nanna... the troubled young lovers find a small armoured submarine on Alibaba and set themselves a quest. PING... Nge'k has the conn, PING... Can't you turn it off... No, it's good.. PING... they chase whales and giant rays through underwater chasms, shred schools of fish in the turbines only to feed smaller fish, torpedo the coral, smash towering thermal vents, every dirty trick turns out fish-food almost ruining the malice. PING-*pinng..* PING-*pinng..* bearing one- six-one.. full ahead, up-scope.. It's only an oil tanker... Wait a minute, what's that... A cruise-ship, we'll be here forever… What's that… Refugees.. and kids… No, that… It's them.. flood both tubes...

8 People driving into town are naive, Mumton belongs to a consortium and boasts a mini-skyline of casinos laundering money, obligated to maintain the private trusts with gross dividends. The annual bar-crawl has beneficiaries drifting custom sedans in memorial, hung-over forty-somethings make their way to renovated clubhouses and office-blocks to relax in quiet groups with offspring of their own in other stories. One kid stays relevant practising dark physics, travels through subspace as he calls it and somehow finds his alternate-reality great-aunt Millie.

The kids new subspace thing's about ready for trials, semi-organic protein-silicate synapses, zinc peptides, it's just a big phone. He'd go but the army's doing everything and they have a test-pilot set to find an attractive inter-dimensional General, a problem with her pension, It's all here in this yellow folder... CLANG… the test-pilot turns to see a kid swinging a heavy Stillson wrench caught on an overhead pipe, he runs two or three steps before it rattles across his back, the kid takes the bloody folder as a credential and using it to hide his face he's hurried onto the pad. There's a strange inverted sound and light drawn to a point, Where'd he go... Is that it… Lock it down.. make back-ups.. looks like it works, Colonel, better tell the President...

That kid likes army life, structure and certainty in an exotic reality, troops yakking about a battle with vampires and packing-up old-time stuff all new with strangely futuristic details. The hot General seems out of place yet very familiar, Who is she... there's rumours, no-one really knows, he shows-up and drops the file on the desk, standard army super, smells of bleach but she doesn't say anything, needs a current postal address, bank details and a signature. He's handing her a pen and recognises his great-aunt Millie in the young General receding decades out of reach, an invisible flash, everything pulsates, bits of nothing decay into grassy fields on a different warm evening, no sense of scale, Where are we... I'm not sure... there's no way to know, it's a paradox, he gives her the pen.

The President breaks from his sketch of the office and wonders why the Colonel's here, It's that weird dimension thing, Sir, there may be something in it... Well fix it, d'you know how much that thing costs... Something behind the concept... So get it the hell out. Do I have to build the damn thing… stops sketching again and looks over his glasses at the Colonel, they discuss subspace coordinates and temporal displacement and keep it quiet but the whole world's talking, dimensional travel's a reality. Korean and Chinese offshore mega-pads dump obsolete goods from somewhere in the near future, prepaid by timely investments in the past and delivered by drone wherever and whenever thanks to paradox-rectifying software.

A guy reaches for a latch and notices a small parcel at his feet, probably left by a drone, looks like a set-up. He steps back down, crosses the street and sees a well dressed woman approach, check her purse and hurry away. The street-lights are coming on, some kids roll up on bikes and race inside, a taxi finally arrives and people come down but no-one picks-up the little box. He gets coffee at the place on the corner, the blonde woman comes back with keys in her hand and a guy meets her on the steps, they have words and he leads her away. There's another taxi with those people tripping and laughing and it's just starting to spit, he turns-up his collar.

Shots ring out in the pouring rain, the fancy blonde runs past carrying her shoes and goes straight inside, he panics and starts toward the all-night café. A dark sedan peels around and screeches to a halt, the door swings open and slams as the heavy town-car fishtails back up the rainy city street.. D'ja get it... Who.. what... Did you get the box... It's on the step back there… What.. how.. shit, reset... We can't do that...

Dry clothes, he's home from work, reaches for the latch and remembers the box, it isn't there, he scrambles but it's still not there, shouts up the street THERE'S NO BOX... a few people turn, sun's shining, traffic's normal, kids playing on the footpath giggle at the crazy man, he goes inside, there's nothing the other side of the door, Yeah I knew we couldn't just do that, things have to coordinate, parallel stuff line-up, fuck-knows where that guy is and there's still no box…

At the same time but deep in the future the holo-monitor shows a blip in a tiny dimension, I think it's the box.. how'd it get in there... the guy mumbles distantly and rotates the image, A rift, Colonel, maybe do-able… the specialists drop in to assess conditions.. it's huge, time's slow and the sky's wrong.. otherwise it's a lot like here. There's that guy, disappeared through that door, Have you seen that box... it's the guys from that car, Yeah, it's in my room. I think it's it.. it's bigger, more like a bag, and it hums. Hey, are you ladies hungry, time's really slow, we could get a beer…

He says it keeps getting bigger and louder but very gradually, Colonel, time's a lot slower here… Damn, they said this might happen.. this could mean the end of everything as we know it, you have to get rid of it… We could drop it some place... That won't do, it has to go, that's an order... they crank the dimension thing way up, hold hands and abandon reason, You too mate, get in here...

A parking cop's writing a ticket, a woman holds her briefcase out stepping off a bus, pedestrians walk past and pigeons fly over. The casino's gloomy and stale with a lunchtime crowd of girls going home and alcoholics having heart-starters. Addicts keep a tight schedule getting-on morning and night, no time to eat, can't sit here all day, where's the guy..

He gets the gear and meets the fading sunset outside, fluid drips in his throat screwing-up his stomach, he's scratching looking harshly up the street, hails a cab and takes a drive-thru.

God, where've you been... she can taste gin, the punk kisses her neck, feels a boob and slips her a satchel of brown rocks, there's people in the lounge, Hey... Hey... her little brother with a bashed-up friend.

Gun-barrel warm from sitting all morning in his mouth when a cold acidic scream draws his attention.. upstairs.. the door with the violence. He shoulders it open, empties his fathers pistol into the guy and tends to the battered girl on the floor, she takes a bag from under the bed and grabs her keys, they push past the shocked neighbours and rush to escape in her car, he knows people, his sister, they can get high and lay-low.

The sister's bad-seed boyfriend steps into the lounge You can't stay here... but he knows a place up the coast, a hollow concrete block anchored into the coarse sand, it goes under in the tide, the entrance twenty meters up the rocks where they never built the upper floors, fully swank with big windows onto the desolate patch of ocean.. the delinquents fit right in.

No, I was robbing the place.. that's his car.. was... the kid wants to say What... but it doesn't seem adequate staring into the bag full of loot.. dad's old revolver and a packet of cigarettes beside it on the bed, he goes Fuck... both dodging school, they have to lie to get alcohol.

9 Birth and Death

Countless tunnels and trains into every darkness with ghosts caught on splinters of forgotten desire, almost tasting real air with ethereal fingers in a long complex moment that sees ejected carriages concertina into a hillside. Fighting for a place in the blood and debris, *sigh...* the wraith is finally whole, dirty and slow.

Familiar but not a memory, deja-vu but current and real, WAAGH.. WAAGH... she may not be entirely alone and there she is crying to herself, a likely source of the echo. She reaches for empirical support and finds a noisy abstract blur, has to trust instinct kicking feebly clenching her tiny fists, she's hungry but it's only hormones, no-one cares about food. Sounds and smells draw close, time stops, she can fly in an intangible world and remembers it's all okay.

She doesn't know she's woken-up in a room flooded with morning light, just goes for a fresh perspective and finds heaviness and stilted movement, the suffocating pace, she so wants to cry but chooses not to and accepts a lifetime of tedium, she's arrived, excitedly waving stiff arms and legs ignoring the clumsiness, hungry again, chooses again not to cry, halved her workload.

Milk and honey at the kindy.. socialising.. the terrified look on that boy when she lifts her skirt. Her friend's at the table with the crayons, they both laugh, she sits and starts to draw, What are you drawing… A horse... I'm doing a giraffe… portrait, yellow crayon, head up there, a long neck and legs down there, big brown spots, black eyes, nose, feet and a little tail, There… holds it up, the other one laughs, she pulls it down for grass along the bottom, blue across the top, There… her friend's taking forever. She resents the pedestrian litany and doesn't remember why, hangs a plum tree in the sky so he'll have something to eat.

Cows say moo, ducks say quack.. a prodigy, A a for apple, Z z for zebra.. it's soon P.K.D. and Hermann Hesse, lunchtime symposiums, philosophic sandwiches, It is… My sandwich, cheese and date... That's not the point, it just is… Wish it was a joint…

O.D.s and suicides most of them, charm wears off and boredom hangs around. Same old dawn except our girl's been looking forward to this very day, counting the sleeps 'til she finally gets shuttle-duty, dock with the toxic waste and fling it at the sun, takes about forty hours and dangerous as hell. Her plan is to drop it back down, she's convincing herself it's a reasonable course, there's no turning back now.. the waste container burns away and radioactive contents vaporise, a mutagenic plague released on innocent chromosomes.

Susie has two heads giggling with the kids at the creche, limbs all over their body, legs growing from their head and much grosser things, it doesn't matter among the asteroids, you find mutants anywhere that holds an atmosphere. Football's hilarious, they could sell tickets if people weren't so stubbornly prejudiced. I like what it's doing to the frogs… These are ants.. you don't want to see the frogs… Looks like they'll be serving ants-legs at the benefit...

Time runs at a leisurely pace on Earth since the free-trade agreement with the mutants, a golden opportunity for some questionable characters, We don't need the mutant trade, what about our jobs… WHAT ABOUT OUR JOBS… rabble are easily roused when they're frightened. Nothing's wrong with pursuing a career apart from the obvious, this guy's executive material, ripe for politics, It's legal in some places… That's a scream, use it at the dinner…

10 Genes naturally-select sprawling with cruel pointless desire, a timeless dog rolling blissfully in rotting corpses, homo-sapiens sapiens runs out to play while his mother goes to forage. Well dressed, solid hips and generous bosoms, stenographer thirty years ago, sixty words a minute, might be a bit rusty, she'll try a few places, You're old.. can you make coffee… name's Doreen, friends call her Doris.

Concerned at a page, her mind racing rifling the files, Wait a minute.. that makes three this month... and brings it up with the girls who quickly change the subject. She studies the file, checks totals and googles the letterhead on the invoices, S. D. C.. *Same Day Cleaners – we'll take care of it...* six figures, they must be good. From her desk she can see the entrance to the S. D. C. offices, buys a telephoto lens and sets- up surveillance on people in dark suits and sunglasses stepping out of matt black muscle-cars, often with an instrument case, could be a recording studio in there.. it explains the federal cops.

That's human, I've seen one before... It's so small, how can it be that loud... and it grows-up so fast, an ordinary teenager out with friends. We don't know just how or when she learns of her mysterious past but it makes a difference, she packs a bag and hits the road without a word to anyone.

A guy has his arms around her holding her hands out in front, You hold it like this.. line it up.. and squeeze... this other guy shows her Shaolin kung-fu and teaches her mad driving skills, good enough for a job with S. D. C. where she takes an office facing the street. Hey, that lady's watching the building.. we should check it out... shadow-warrior along the footpath and drop silently through a skylight.

Someone's in the hall, she acts natural, stilettos the guy and dumps the body in a maintenance cupboard.. here comes the janitor.. little smile, nod, and when he opens the door she slams a combat-knife through his neck, rips-out his throat and piles the body onto the other one, moves along the hall to the second from the end and takes Doris in a Chinese death-lock mobilising the head with twenty-two kilos pressure snapping the spine at the C 3-4 junction, the subject's paralysed but the brain lives for a few minutes. The cool killer takes her time pulling the memory card and wiping the hard-drive, Why the telephoto lens... no answer, staring at the floor, drool, tears, the assassin spins the chair and demands Why are you watching us... I'm in love with your boss... slap slap.. Who are you working for... Your mother... she takes the stapler and begins savagely beating the helpless old lady, her heart breaking with every blow, What do you know about my mother... she lurches sobbing from the room leaving Doris at her desk paralysed and bleeding, watches the bodies on their way to the morgue and wonders about the family she never knew.

11 Mankind reaches again for the stars, something better click this time, people still hurt from the cruel mutant-wars and we haven't seen any aliens since the plague. Saturn's posted as a resort colony, a wide

selection of moons, sirens on Titan and rings as far as you can see it sounds magical, and not cheap, the private venture dominates the news, articles read like pamphlets.

A pensive mood settles in elevators and lunch-rooms turning quickly to agitation, a rush on the pawnshops infectious progressing to panic and terror, busses overturned and set alight, garbage bins through shop windows.. teargas.. looting.. shots fired.. we agree to hold a lottery and all someday win a terrace on a Saturn moon.

Jeanie, have you seen my cami… No, and call me Eva… Yeah why… Evgenya, I love that name... Okay Evgenya, have you seen the red camisole… Yeah I said no, where was it… they'll talk about anything to fill the chapters in a pointless existence that'll surely change once they finally get off this rock.

Nothing ever changes much for this guy studying insignificant wows and flutters in the magnetic field, with records going back years. He's on a laptop at a table when Eva and her friend spot him Hey, he's cute… Looks like a lunatic… Yeah, I like the crazy ones… she leaves Eva at the bar, What'll it be, Jean… It's Evgenya... Okay, what'll you have… Vodka of course, with lime… With lime.. ice?.. Yeah, thanks… Pretty name, Evgenia… Evgenya… Sorry, Slovenian eh...

The other one's realising why that cute guy's alone, she joins Eva, Beer thanks, and a shot of single-malt… Stewy was saying he'd like to fix the place up a bit… Good idea, Stu, *throw money out the window*.. another shot of that scotch thanks… Great isn't it, it's Japanese… Me too thanks, and pour one for yourself… why not, they could lift-off at any moment.

These girls are very old when they notice a big yellow envelope slide under the door and a knock but there's nobody by the time they get there, one gets up, shuffles toward the entrance and takes a break leaning on her walker, then bend, retrieve the envelope, stand back up and breathe, open the door, nobody there, and shuffle back, What is it… I don't know, gimme a minute… sounds like a steam-engine pulling-up stressing the furniture, fat old fingers mauling the package, rip.. spilling the contents across the table onto the floor. You get it, it's on your side… she has to get down to pick the stuff up and climbs painfully back onto the chair, Can I have the glasses… Giv'us a look… Just give me the damn glasses, please... finds her own in her apron, it's the stupid Saturn thing, Wow, it's that Saturn thing...

Down by the docks a guy manages to gasp Ask yourself.. what would.. Jesus do… He'd probably ask you again who's cutting the merchandise.. Oomph... in the guts, the guy slumps, bile runs down into the blood on his shirt, stooges prop him up while goons work him over, Give our guest bucket-boots and show him the aquarium... That's three this month, we could shuffle the territories… Now that's why I keep you around, you got ideas and you're ambitious.. c'mon, I'll buy dinner… Not tonight, I got a date… diving for cover and reaching for holsters as a gold Chevy Nova rounds the corner, ouzis peek-out and brazenly strafe the footpath with .45s blasting back, LUNCH… from behind a van, YEAH.. I'LL BRING CAROL… hunched behind a ute, on a razors edge, they'd probably be safer as spies and there may be more money but crime runs in families, similar lifestyle except for the Aston-Martin budget and it's no secret, drugs and prostitutes, Listen, kid... between courses at the restaurant, Don't worry about money, we got you covered, an' them secrets is just paper trails and old photos… shop-talk, Carol and Doll-Face go powder their nose with the girls cutting rails on the dresser, mini-bar at the end, piped catwalk music, women having sex on the seats. The goon at the door has an earpiece, it's time to go, the girls return and we help them with their coats So we're good, yous'll think about it, right… Yeah.. we'll talk it over… Talk what over, babe… Opportunity, honey, this could be our break.. how do you feel about Saturn...

12 A barely perceptible dip generates a sharp gasp in the passengers as rockets take the weight, Sorry about that, folks… the captain's reassuring tone.. Touching down in three.. two.. one… cheering turns to quiet awe as airlock doors slide open onto rolling hills of vapour in a soft blue light.

The old ladies are in walkers waiting for the lift at the cargo door looking down at an alien tarmac, nice blue lawn and very soft blue light coming through the hatch, Blue… Yes, lovely, and so soft…

Yeah, real fragile... Yes, fragile… mixed feelings until they see the resort mildewed and crumbling every bit a hundred years old, a mushroom-vine's taken over, looks like a jungle and it's all the same blue fungus. We all turn, surprised and betrayed at the sound of the ship leaving, people sigh audibly, a baby cries.. probably a coincidence.

Golf-courses, water-parks and luxury villas are all still here, dioramas and green- screens in the broken-down foyer of a derelict structure, lights and camera equipment still roughly in place, the magnitude weighing in, Can you eat the mould… I'd wait 'til we see someone.. let's spread-out…

Elevators spring to life, lights hum and it's distracting but they settle down, ventilators start up, climate control, HELLO… sound doesn't carry, Absorbed by all the blue… It's just humid, quit moaning, I'll bet everyone's on the roof…

You can see for miles from up here, the same blurry carpet in every direction. Great effect… Weird… IT'S THE SPORES.. DON'T BREATH THEM IN… we move away from the edge. Someone's stepping from the mould, scrappy beard and dirty bare feet, loud and sure, I don't like him but it's probably good advice, I hope we don't have to talk to this guy, Where is everyone...

Not many survived the spores, I think we're immune, a couple on the hill over there and some up north in caves… That hill just there... I'm dreaming, we'll never get the walkers across, Is there a bus... You could take the old jump-car if it still works but they'd have to fire-up the receptor-coils at the other end, I'll send a text.. yep, they'll have it on tomorrow.. that gives us a few hours to get this thing in shape, be careful not to touch any spores...

Saturn's slipped from the headlines, the nieces are getting worried, it may be nothing but nobody's heard anything, they've almost stopped sending ships and no-one's allowed on the ones that go. We've got to get on board one of those ships... Get guys to go… hug the wall under the cameras, time it right and slip aboard while they unload mysterious sealed pallets.

Blue-stained zombies sniff deeply at an open crate, sometimes taking a handful and eating it, Mate… the guys sneak around and take a good sniff, dig their hands in and have a bight, the mistakes merging into something catastrophic, they manage to stuff their shirts and escape undetected.

Spores take hold in the damp soil around the drains, blue fungus breaks into the plumbing diverting the water through conduits of its own, we're soon part of its inter dimensional web in an open multiverse. Realities emerge nothing like each other, one's a sort of negative-space slowly changing and might be two dimensional, I wonder what that's like and a low voice hums It's all the same as itself… the texture changes two-dimensionally and the place breaks-up into slabs, each with a slightly different reflection. I don't know which one's me, they all are, the perspective changes moving through the mirrors shifting in an unfamiliar way positioning here and there, opening different futures from each new reflection, we could get lost. We all turn and cross the room conscious of the others doing the same into different futures, and from respective lounges watch the last few slabs fold like a sheet and disappear.

I'm not drinking any more of that water and empty the glass into the mouldy sink, there's vodka and beer in the fridge, whisky on the table, we hold rowdy meetings developing a plan for bio-domes free from the mould. A society of fungicidal maniacs grows from there and pretty-quickly reclaims the planet.

Everyone loves living here, dodging elephants and chasing-off packs of wild dogs SHOO... a woman flaps a towel at them and they back away more annoyed than intimidated, no-one growls or snaps. Bloody wolves… the comment directed at her deceased husband, she doesn't expect a reply but sighs kicking off her shoes just as she always has, sits in her spot and picks-up the centrally placed remote.

Watching her stories in guilty pleasure she catches the news in catholic penance.. *packs of wild dogs roaming the streets...* there's a shot of them sniffing around, *..and once elected he'll address this and many other urban problems...* she flicks the channel, ads, ads, news, the same news as the other channel, more ads, hey, the movie channel, a sci-fi classic, Planet of the Apes.. Fuck-off… Damn you all to hell… the ghost quips silently from the end of the lounge, she's pretty-drunk laughing switching channels, footy, it can't be too bad, it's very popular.. a guy catches a ball and runs straight into this other guy, they may run into each other, she can't say.

They keep doing that but it's never obvious who runs into whom, then those guys have the ball running into these guys and it's clear the one's with the ball do most of the running. It's good for about twenty minutes and she catches herself nodding-off, the news has ended, she's scrolling through the channels with renewed interest, cop shows.. a crusty but very attractive lawyer.. a movie about cops.. ooh, an environment doco, This Bitter Earth… haven't seen it *Yechh*… she's confronted with an image that almost curdles the plasma screen, the horror progressing with each vile frame, viewers of all ages wail and claw their eyes, vomit into their dinner, throw it at the TV but miss peering through tears of helplessness and rage. The show is archived, top-shelf never-to-be-seen where it finds its way into a weapons lab.

The widow's clutching her stomach switching the channel, a zombie movie and it's really good. She hates scary movies, too scared to go close the door so it's swinging randomly banging and creaking, she pulls-up the doona and buries into the pillow, if she shut the door she could switch-on the light but can't do any of that petrified on the lounge, can't reach for the remote in case there's a zombie under the table waiting to grab her arm, it might be standing right behind her, she pulls the covers up watching the gory movie through a fold jumping when the door bangs, a familiar condition fresh every time.

The bike's hard to start but it goes when it gets going, she's going red from kicking it, doesn't ride it as much as she should and it roars into life filling the garage with throbbing. She looks great in leathers peeling out into the street. sold the Harleys when the old-man died, got a British bike and a '66 Mustang, loves the Shooting Star though it takes a lot of attention and can be hard to start, only rides it to the airport, has a spot in the hanger with a hook for the helmet. She likes being rich, straight into the very expensive booze on the private jet,

Where we going… Guatemala… Where the fuck is Guatemala.. is that near Guam... No smoking in the cockpit, please, we'll be there in a minute, sit down and fasten your seat-belt… It goes very well, they'll keep doing whatever they do and she'll keep getting richer.

On her way home drinking the tiny bottles in the Limo when she learns of a problem with the plane, they have to stay-over in a seedy motel. It's okay until they see the room, there must be something better, The guy in el grande hacienda might give you a room... they call from the car, very comfortable turning through the gate into an immaculate driveway made for the stretched white Limo.

They're greeted warmly by someone in gloves and led into the opulent drawing room, BUENOS DIA, muchachitas.. mi casa su casa… a fat balding little guy in a white suit fills the place with enthusiasm, the foreign widow wobbles holding out her hand, he kisses it and she drops back into the chaise Hola, signor, I'm sorry, who are you… I am Manuel Rodriguez el Cordoba… he looks incredulously at his guest, I know you, senora.. rather, I knew your late husband. He once gained from me something I very much desire returned, perhaps you know of it, a brooch, gold, like that one, also mounted with the blackest of diamonds, and yes, I see clearly seven sapphires forming a deep blue cluster.. porfavor, where did you get this piece… It was my husband's, he gave it to me,

I've always hated it and wear it as a symbol of living with him always hogging the remote, watching the news, I couldn't catch my stories it was unbearable, this hideous brooch is perfect and means a lot to me… Unfortunate, my dear, to be so attached to something that does not belong to you, perhaps you could be compensated… Thanks, we noticed a lovely helicopter on the lawn… Si, los Quetzalcoatl, she is yours as a token of good-will between our families… he goes to kiss her hand, she pulls it away And those alpacas, I'd like them at my place to chase the wild dogs… You cannot take Mehitabel and Tomasina but you shall have your guard- camels with my blessing… grabs her hand and kisses it, she ceremoniously hands-over the brooch, Gracias, senora, enjoy your stay, if there's anything you need.. JAVIER... he's leaving with his prize as Javier steps back in to show them to the guest house.

13 Policy

I don't know Jim very well, seems alright, maybe preoccupied with personal hygiene but that can't be a bad thing, I don't know what he wants, the movies he watches, emotional issues, probably a story in itself, the magical world of books.

There's also a girl, likes low-budget independent movies and raw garage-band punk, didn't want to come to the beach with the dorks from work. The water's freezing and full of seaweed, she wades-out waist deep and stands not getting her hands wet, alone, everyone back on shore waving and shouting excitedly TURN AROUND… it's too late, the fin disappears underwater as a big shark makes a run at her but misses by a few feet, she bobs under into the masses of kelp and it's right there, she grabs his nose and slips back to hold onto the dorsal fin while he thrashes around, gets a good grip with both hands, she can steer by twisting and guides him onto the beach. Gee, you're lucky… but that's more than just luck, Jim's been studying unusual phenomena, there's often a simple explanation, this is clearly a matter of attitude.

He sometimes wonders about that girl but doesn't care enough to look her up, he's pursuing a career and has responsibility to protect. Nice digs, a car, he bought a hat but doesn't think he'll wear it, no-one knows the real Jim, he's just that very clean guy who dresses well.. whatever anyone thinks it's not him, he's doesn't identify with anything and wishes he could do more.

Chaos is the natural state, it's why there's no superheroes, we could have robots much more powerful than a train, running-down speeding bullets, leaping tall buildings no problem. Early ones always look like refrigerators, then girl-shaped ones of course, smaller and sexier with Manga costumes, some pretty funky weapons that quickly develop into standard lightening-bolts from their fingers and laser-beam eyes, rocket-boots, maybe a dance mode.

It doesn't matter why dinosaurs did anything, art so esoteric we accept it as nature, Balancing Rocks.. Waterfalls.. Big Holes in Mountain-

Sides.. very popular in their time, probably had their shit poets and writers, you can't force it, humans will be painting really nice ochre inside the Big Holes and completely change the aesthetic, give it scale we can relate to and a familiar theme of violence and exploitation, we were so young. We're more closely related to a dinosaur than to an alien, do we put them on the table or just ignore them, it could mean war with the football-shaped beings from another world. I sit down beside them and they roll across up onto my lap, I hope it's not sexual but who doesn't want to bang an alien, I'm getting okay with it and they start biting my arms, taking little chunks so I stand-up and brush them off.

They make a low menacing sound rolling in my direction, an attractive xenomorph steps-in with an electronic dog-whistle and pulls them into line. Hi… in a very sexy off-world tone, I check her out and lick my lips as I imagine a porn-star might, Hel-lo… but for inter- species relationship you'd have to go mammal, a seal maybe, something warm, a tiger with some cute little cubs. A zoo is the safest option, vets on hand and a controlled environment but it could be expensive. People have old pets they're bored with and might welcome someone taking an interest, bringing them dinner and a fresh blanket, get each others mood and growl attentively, read to them but they're asleep after two pages, maybe catch a wilderness movie..

14 People file onto the bus, Oh, is that her… no, it's not her, and a few people later There she is… no, and that's everyone, Michael looks hopefully back as they pull into traffic but there's no sign of her. Of course he wonders where she is, he's biting his lip looking down at his hands and glances in despair out the window, she's busy getting married in six weeks but he doesn't know anything about it.

She's there tomorrow and he's resolved to introduce himself, kept a seat and indicates to her to climb up. Hi, I'm Michael… Hello Michael, thanks for keeping the seat… an attractive Turkish accent, she's clearly charmed and he blushes Oh that's alright, what's your name… her name's Lila, she lives around here, works at the supermarket and no, she's not a goat she's an Angora and very clear on that. She nibbles his hair This is my stop, see you Michael... he's planning the rest of his life, more a projection than a plan, a day-dream that lasts all the way to school.

They never speak again, she bleats and he blushes if their eyes ever meet, a few weeks later she stops catching the bus. Michael.. MICHAEL.. damn that kid always day-dreaming... Ray charges heatedly across the lawn carrying a spade like a rifle, mum running beside him clutching his arm almost copping an elbow, Calm down, Ray, don't do this... sobbing and falling about but Ray remains resolute, never liked young Michael and this is his chance to do some damage, a few deft blows with the shovel sees the end of the kid. You've done it now, Ray, they'll be looking for you... he knows it all too well, throws bushes over the boy's mutilated body and races for the train, a cross-country freight passes through and he means to be on it.

Skulking between shadows is time-consuming, it's coming-up midnight, he jacks a car and goes speeding down back-lanes, straight through lights, one-way streets, he doesn't seem to care, flushed and sweating, collar turned up and a stubble beard, all the time checking his watch, checking the mirrors, he can see the tracks on his left, hears a whistle blowing and puts his foot down, he'll drive along side and jump across just before it hits..

A brilliant full-moon hides the smaller stars and exposes the few clouds, someone's out walking with a camel. Ray doesn't see them until it's too late, he swerves sharply, the car flips a few times and he dies just as the train rolls past still blowing the whistle.

15 Used to be grass as far as you could see, all under a mile of micro-plastics now, the last few ice-ages really moved that stuff around. The dirt is toxic confetti, home to select species of grubs and beetles, we're here to maintain the antique geothermal equipment ionising gasses to run fuel-cells. A few weeks does my social obligation for another year, economics no longer driving production, we're all proud of what we make, it's a contribution, these fuel cells are shipped across the system powering the wonderful inter-planetary civilisation.

Augmented reality unites the colonies simultaneously with paired-ion-communication, P.I.C, and the interface is so good you can't tell unless your active contact lenses break or your chip goes off-line, the LEDs and phosphor coatings are real so the appearance doesn't change much but you lose holograms and A.I.s, get no data stream or kinetics, you might as well not be there.

People sleeping everywhere, I don't know where the masses crowding the streets come from, a wall-to-wall population that shuffles between recreation and sleep enslaved by the new world order. Everything's free if you can find something but you don't need anything, free booze and generic drugs, sex with a public robot, eat at civic meal-stations and maybe find somewhere to sleep.

A bus is coming, people can't get out of the way, I don't know how many are killed but it makes no dent in the crowd smearing blood and body-parts along the street, here comes another free bus, this may have been alright for our parents but it's about time we took some action.. install pedestrian crossings and no-sleeping zones.

.. a glass will smash.. SMASH… *that guy walks past..* and sure enough the guy walks past, she remembers the curtains catching fire with flames spreading through the dining-room and moves toward the door but it's not deja vu, she sees the future, some twists and turns and it's cops on hover-bikes, women on ebay, comets flying past and a big planet with rings filling the sky, nothing seems important anymore.

Sure it's colourful, probably gets the trophy, the narrow focus is a give-away but no-one seems to mind, it's pretty and that always gets awards no matter how crude, Elegant for something so gross, I like what they've done with the immersive interface, it all just seems a bit arbitrary... prospective parents debate the issues, choosing a spot to raise a family can be crucial, things to consider they can't imagine laying groundwork for remorse, so many potential generations resting on the decision.

Ancestors make all the choices they can, how many arms, how many legs, how tall, skinny, it must be a nightmare putting the genetic template together, probably a matter of balance, everything to scale, little spiders, big whales. Big lizards was a good idea at the time, a compromise in factors implemented way before anything, technical stuff older than dirt, before quantum-physics or entanglement, struggling with sound, setting the periodic table for molar entropy, we're lucky the lights work.

16 Existence is an assault and every living thing should be duly compensated by the church, creation without certification or liability-cover should itself mean a class action backdated to the year zero in perpetuity for every shitty thing that happens.

It's all up to the judge, the church admits God made everything and as appointed representatives they assume liability, atheists insist the church is only guilty of taking advantage but should face punitive damages for that, the judge can't possibly care, that'd be crazy. Tossing a coin is unprofessional, maybe hold a race, make them fight, these are terrible ideas, he goes to bed finding no relief in sleep, dreams of people cutting bits off themselves, hitting him with the pieces and vomiting on him, wakes in sweat gasping for breath, has coffee and heads back to work. Doesn't like the church and the atheists have surprisingly similar smug self-righteous arguments, either way the church has to pay but that can't influence any decision.

God gets recognition for His work on existence and takes full responsibility for any subsequent hardship pursuant to municipal and state private or civil liability code. Mysterious parcels explode on the doorstep, menacing calls increase dramatically, his wife's not safe and the kids are at grandma's, the judge wincing turning the key expecting the car to explode and the other one bursts into flame. He wonders if them losing means he wins by default.. they did blow-up a car so that's one for them, and from their perspective he was in the wrong one.. he can't stop judging, it's his life, it drives the family crazy, mum wanted to go with the kids but stayed in danger and spends her time cowering, glad the car didn't explode, You'd be better-off on the seat, darling, not much ever comes through the roof and you can be crushed by the motor down there... Can you stop judging me for one second... she's had enough, wishes he never took that job, it didn't even pay much, thirty pieces of silver, not enough to get them out of the mess it made.

Better than a bag of salt or a goat but not as good as his weight in gemstones.. the judge judging value in different types of exchange ignoring his strong commercial bias, inherent racism and misogyny, secretly gay, repressed and bitter.

I'd shoot anyone for the smile on somebody's face, the laughter of a child payment enough, better than any number of sunsets or associated meteorological phenomena and I'm BLAM… it may be a random hit, I don't know who shoots him or why but we won't be hearing any more from that guy except by Ouija board.

Very little's known about poltergeists and it's a shame as there's one right outside, it's so scary, the temperature drops but we smoke too much to close the window, a vase tips and smashes violently on the floor, all hell's about to break loose.. nothing.. then the curtain lifts and a few people jump, not much of a menace. We're new and the horrors of the dark-side are sure to deepen with practice, dark practice, mumbling in Sumerian over stuff in a cauldron, boiling frogs toes and a lizards eye, never thought we'd be doing this, *pfoof…* a twisted face silently screaming rises from the brew although everyone sees it differently, some say a rabbit, maybe, something..

A guy's hooked-up to a battery and we're running tests getting no results.. there should at least be something.. an electrical anomaly's interfering with the equipment, there's no way to test for that, we can only speculate and get straight to it, nothing's outside the realms of the unknown, it may just be a flat battery, this is pointless.. we gave it a good shot.. and it's been fun.. but..

No.. wait.. something's coming-up on one of the dials, Pip.. Pip.. Pip.. this other thing starts beeping flashing a light, the dial drops back to zero, the beeping stops but the light keeps flashing, people are losing interest BOOM… all the lights come on, some bulbs explode and a thunderous voice smashes the TV, pushes-out the doors and deafens everyone. Nobody gets what it says, it never repeats and it's all over in an instant but lasts forever in the hearts of the witnesses and raises occult doubts with no place in this world, darkness waiting or brooding.. I don't know anymore.

17 Something might be missing I can't put my finger on, an unseen factor that lends cosmic relevance to these moments, provides some context for the incessant rotation, it could be anything, most likely a ubiquitous immeasurably faint field, a pervasive impossibly-thin fabric of dark force.

I don't know what the crowd makes of it but no-one's laughing, they're all just standing around vaping drinking white wine in agreement ignoring the elephant in the room, the dark force not being in space just in the same place coinciding with space pulling strings to build this decaying moment from nothing. It has to be a lever, or a fulcrum, I'm not an engineer, but it's clearly a third-party to the space and energy.

No-one ever thinks they might be dark matter, wouldn't notice time missing always doing, will do and having done everything apparently all at once, it's not something they think about. Time's an idea for them, it takes less than a moment to investigate turning-up no evidence, there may be space with time passing but nothing could live there, a chaotic stream of events with arbitrary cohesion. They're mostly ambivalent on the subject, an opinion that needn't exist, it divides them in a timeless civil war. They've suddenly killed all they ever will, voiced and resolved objections, painted slogans and erased them all in the same instant, there's only one moment and this is it, no-one gives a shit about time but it's no longer ambivalence.

Sooner or later it all comes back to normal reality, a trans-dimensional hover-car, the kid driving must be about twelve, I'd guess he's stolen it. A gang of kids in the car drinking great coffee with a conspicuous older couple, getting a lift to the nexus.. Thanks… Cool… the kids could go to any dimension from here and this car has everything built in. They're going as deep as they can to the far reaches of existence, gauges redlining when they hit the solid-state boosters, the car slips into a place it shouldn't and falls straight back out, Wow… the kids are tapping icons and swiping but don't seem to be moving.. they've blown the dimension card.

They're forced to steal another car, delete most of it to save space in the buffer, won't need a fridge, or a toaster, they strip it right back, ninety-eight percent of the cpu running dimension software in many vain attempts, it's almost as if something's blocking them. The kids drift apart, the memory fades and distorts, starting to rationalise.. a trick of the quantum light, inter-dimensional swamp gas, it both did and didn't happen.. the idea's lost for all time although there was once a future where they confirmed the bold discovery bringing an entire age of understanding to its own destruction by paradox.. they somehow block their past selves and never exist, not many cultures are still capable of time-manipulation.

18 It's Alive

That's a Bower Bird, they all sing in the morning, pretty as hell, evenings too, and there's lots of animals.. wallabies.. wombats.. an echidna came in for a drink while we filled the water-thing.. yeah, cute.. limited resources, the sense of loss.. pfff, wildlife, it's all around, nothin' too bad, spiders and snakes, no bears or anything, possums, and rats like guinea-pigs with tails, and there's ferals, abandoned pets, farm refugees.. no, you should like the place…

These new people love it, Is that a Brown Snake… It'll be an adder or a taipan… No bears, right dad… That's what he said, son… the kids heard him say spiders and they know just where they might be.. the hunt's on for the biggest live funnel-web, DON'T GO TOO FAR… not far enough yet. The spiders hear them coming, fangs designed to pierce flesh are poised dripping powerful venom OW… it really hurts, MUM.. SOMETHING BIT TOMMY… he's gone in three minutes TOMMY… mum's crying, dad grumbling about caskets and taxes. People arrive way too late, the patient's unresponsive, dad files for litigation but spiders were mentioned at the walk-through, another round of despair and it's all over. Tom's just the first to fall, next goes dad then mum but they're old by then, and some time later even Eloise, the house sits empty until the bulldozers move-in.

Car-parks cover the whole reclaimed swamp area with a shopping mall where the old place stood but not in living memory, forgetting about the spiders OW… impressive fangs and rich toxins find their mark, could be a problem, they hurry the old lady into the back and give her a chair behind some boxes, bring her some water and hold her hand. They'll drop the body from the roof, make it look like an accident, she must have wandered up there, sounds good.. raises eyebrows with the paramedics but she's old and has no family, the Public Liability cheque is quietly distributed among department heads. Vagrants start leaping from the building, homeless kids blast fire-extinguishers into their own mouth probably trying to get high, all with the same lucrative result, stretched cars all 'round and none of them even like cars.

The universe doesn't mind until they start calling each other Babe, take-downs and arrests take a few minutes but hang in the news and start the collapse of an entire retail empire, the insurance guys are really angry, their only recourse is to have them erased and arrange for some cleaners to take care of it. No mercy for the shop guys, nature can't stand them, they keep getting lost, break-out in sores, birds shit on them, it can't get any worse then they're mercilessly gunned-down, the chemicals find lower energy states releasing the difference as heat.

19 *Events erupt like blisters on the surface of existence…* Kevin writes weird shit and can't resist this.. the tablet's open at his sister's face-book page, she's forgotten it.

KEVIN, get off your sisters computer… they're leaving town in a hurry, can't wait for her, god they hope she's alright. She's with the cheer-squad who wonder why the kids are sitting there Hello… like she's answering a phone, Hi… giggling with Reyna, safe among the big girls, sharing a screen, she left her tablet at home.. Kevin better not be using it *We interrupt this garbage to advise everyone still in the Mid-Central area the time to evacuate has passed and you must seek shelter immediately…* hysteria takes a minute to develop. There's an abandoned fallout shelter under the football field but the big girls don't mention it, resolved to die where they stand defiantly smoking and drinking, the kids crawl abject and sobbing under the stadium and find a miracle door to an enchanted bunker. The cheerleaders push past on the stairs and flick on the lights, those bastard guys must have skipped town so it's all tiny outfits, pom-poms and two kids in a five-acre cold-war palace.

Giant screens light-up with old movie clips, swirling colours and fresh techno beats, the kids get the news on Reyna's tablet, *This is a recording.. everyone's dead.. repeat.. this is a recording…* that's all, it's confusing, We're dead... Yeah, they said everyone… I'm confused… It's weird… they can't bring themselves to tell the others all laughs and smiles, it's hard to watch but they catch a few routines, Reyna's very interested, Just us now, eternally most likely, by all accounts… Yeah, I think so.. unless you're summoned by some Dark-

Lord... Anyway, together in here and I don't mind, what about you... Well, I.. let's just see what happens...

That's nothing, this guy crashes his car through the rail along the cliff, the air-bags go off and he slams into the ground... Shit, is he alright... No, of course he dies, but the air-bags, it's funny... No it's not... Yeah, it's ironic... it might be the wrong story for this girl, Hey, have you ever ridden a horse... JACKSON, would you please get rid of this guy... Jackson's not here to make friends but doesn't just want to hurt people, he likes to humiliate, probably abused as a child, wants to hurt people, it breaks his boyfriends heart. You're better than this... I'm exactly this, Doug, I'm goin' to the pub... Well.. so am I.. a different one... *a different one*, the words cut him even now, DOUG... Jackson cries in his head mentally wrenching his shirt with real passion, then back to work protecting these rich kids, he takes his place across from Karl at the door.

Karl's okay, he's union watching for violations.. sporting organisations.. political groups.. he blocks the doorway and takes-out a bus-load of footy fans, the video'll be a scream. Jackson filters the crowd.. ugly jacket.. ears too big.. hair too neat, they're the worst, and polyester.. he's just dicking around, nods at Karl and goes to check the kids, here's Doug to pick him up from work half an hour early, it's so sweet but it means he'll miss the video of Karl bouncing all those dorks.. he smiles and waves.

Isn't that a WW2 bomber... It's a gay fishing boat, the Smiles And Waves, gets swordfish and crabs out on the Grand Banks... Oh yeah, Worlds Worst something... Yeah those guys, low-budget TV, why don't we do one, People at Keyboards who Can't Type for Shit... Worst Coffee... Yeah but a tele-novella with cars.. and women.. a sexy lady in a nice car.. she parks it well on the first try, lights a cigar and climbs out flashing underpants, Carol.. Carol... she's blindly calling out. Carol's with their best friend, the heartbreak and tension deepen with Carol and the other girl kissing just around the corner, they smell the cigar but stay quiet, a nasty smirk, we're powerless.. cut to commercial...

20 Put it away.. PUT IT AWAY... as if the horror needs emphasis, the doctor leaves the grossly disfigured baby exposed and glares at the Colonel, She's not the only one... resting his hand on the crib he spits-out There's millions of them... again directed at the old Colonel, no-one gets it, it can't be his fault, they're in the office and pretty stoned when the old guy suggests shooting. The drunk doctor quotes something out of context and explains It's us, don't you see.. genetics, horses feet... What horses feet... the Army isn't much on biology.

I warned 'em, told 'em to use an aqueous medium but they wanted gelatinous.. used it in everything, organ transplants, I.V.F.. even gene-splicing... he's sobbing into his elbow and pounding weakly on the desk, Those damn fools, I warned them... but the Colonel still doesn't understand.

We traced the specific sequence to a horse-stud in Queensland, Australia... the doc slumps back to recount the sad tale, I told 'em.. I said Don't do it... Yeah we got that, don't do what... I.V.F, it was crazy, they were putting the stuff right into the gametes, horse-foot genes found a place in the human genome and now... You mean we're all gonna have feet like that freak in the nursery... it's the new normal, we're the freaks. We're a dying race, Colonel.. on the way out...

Both sides go for numbers, the beginnings of Procreative-Action.. the first truly great human war marked by stock and property booms, lots of sex and zero violence, we can never go back we've grown so much, one world, one people with different feet, no countries, no money, cooperating united, but not here.. once the Colonel realises the situation he thinks guns.

You can't shoot genes... the doc waves his hands dismissing the idea and takes his place at the white-board, *Miniature marines with tiny M16s.. blasting away at just the right genes.. then shit them out with all the beans...* referencing Dr Seuss, he's drawn a diagram, thinks he might be heavy on the sarcasm and the Colonel loves the idea, nanobots and microscopic bullets, puts top people on it, they can grow the little buggers in gelatin, Does it have to be gelatin... Afraid so, Colonel, the prostitutes took all the aqueous gel...

A lot of the nanites have keratin shells but it doesn't affect their performance shooting as straight as any mini-robot blasting away in the cell picking off just the right genes. Some start blowing up the chromosomes and the others join right in, they take-over the cells and learn to cooperate forming an e-man far superior to anything organic. That'd be it except for the questionable feet. They experiment with ball-bearings, magnets, rockers & springs and different types of actuator.

Stop thrashing that child, she's just a little girl for crissakes... Show him your damn feet, Sasquatch... belts her again, stamps his horse-foot but she skips aside crying big tears raising a tattered skirt to reveal perfect little feet, Put 'em away, sweetheart... Twenty ducats for the girl, no more... She's yours, Gov', good riddance... she lives happily in a place where everyone has lovely feet, that guy breeds them and sells kids at twenty-five ducats with a clear margin. Soft toes are trending on nearly every menu with demand growing on a dwindling supply, silicone feet start appearing on catwalks and billboards, fit right over your hoof, toes moulded in, Walkers if you have to walk and Posers if you just want to sit, Two sets of Walkers thanks, four sets of Posers... this pimp looks after his girls.

21 Another car swerves off the edge along Cliff Road, the old couple following don't notice and behind them is the start of a cavalcade.. bikes, Humvees, then the Limo and a few S.U.V.s, you can't miss it, takes-up a whole city block, the senator's in there with a prostitute and can't stop every time someone drives over a cliff. The car coming the other way is a V.W. with five big drunk women and only two have a top on then there's nothing for a while.

The highway's always quiet this time of night, a couple of cars go past and a heavy truck carrying a skinny hitch-hiker, You got any family... No, it's just me... Must have a girlfriend... Nah... Well, I've got to pull-in here for a minute, just sit there... he's trying to be casual reaching under the seat, searching with growing impatience for the revolver, Looking for this... grinning stupidly the skinny hitch-hiker braces against the door and shoots splattering the highway-killer in his own cab with his own gun, wow, didn't think he'd ever get that, he posts a selfie and checks his messages *..murder or have sex with someone who's been in space in the last year…*

A car comes past with the interior light on, maybe checking a map, there's a series of random vehicles before a worked Lamborghini streaks through attracting the law, You were doin' a hundred and twenty in a fifty… Well yeah, it's a Lamborghini… the cops are very understanding with naked women and let her go with an ogling. A cadre of ageing bikers rolls past at the speed-limit wary of the patrolling fuzz, there has to be a tail-light or bald tyre in this lot when an urgent call comes over .. *ALL UNITS*… the gang stops at the beach anyway, a few beers, a puff and they're on their way. The cops come screaming past in the other direction with the sun rising on joggers and cyclists, people walking dogs, a few bums still asleep. The beach reaches the base of the cliff with only one car-wreck today, the bodies crushed inside.

The coroner can't believe it, That's Peggy Eckerley… the assistant absently repeats Peggy Eckerley… Yeah, Peggy Eckerley.. *oogly boobly, shakada shake*.. the old guy shakes his shoulders but the kids no wiser, And this is Annie Frangipani, she was on Top of the Pops… Yeah, the Frangipani Sisters, they're great, Annie and Angie… Hey, there's kids here.. don't know who they are… Black one's probably Annie's… the coroner sighs, Giv'us a hand would ya'… it's sensitive work and a crowd's gathering, traffic's picking-up, it's a complex recovery situation, they're forced to expedite with improvised amputations and extricate a bit at a time, THEY WERE ALREADY DEAD, FOLKS, ALREADY DEAD… does little to quiet the protests, a bloody sand-encrusted stump flexing at the lifeless knee, you'd think they've never seen a leg, Get those fingers, Mick.. and grab those soiled clothes, CAN'T LEAVE ANY BEHIND… glancing at the crowd for approval.

Traffic's thick in both directions but I've lost interest, some fluffy clouds appear and there's birds, Think it'll rain… Not unless they're ahead of a front… the worst cyclone the region's ever faced, That's a super-cell, it'll join together, you watch, it's a perfect storm… Piss-off Thompson, you always say that… It is.. look… Hey yeah… Well I'll be damned… you can hear the bated breath as weather-systems merge and there, textbook, no-one ever thought they'd see one, A super-fucking-cell… so excited it doesn't sound stupid at all, they're taking screen-shots to sell to the networks, could make a poster, 3D postcards, Thompson muffles a smirk, they push past him at the keyboard and he's running a scene from a disaster movie, the smile shifts.

Pressure continues to drop, loose objects are flying around, trees bent to breaking are pulled-up by the roots and thrown along the street, a lady pushing a pram lifted and hurled out to sea with a girl on a bike and an old guy with his dog, a heavy storm surge taking their place, four meters deep right where they stood and still coming in, Get a crew out there… loaded with equipment, satellite link and just one brief message *tchht*.. WOAa.. Eeeee.. cuts off mid-scream, wind's howling, Quick, call someone… this is the only building intact.

There's a bottle of old single-malt they've been saving for just such an occasion.. it's probably behind some books, I don't notice exactly where it comes from, a great scotch, liquid velvet, with a box of fine Bolivas.. and out come the darts.. Closest to the bullseye... Highest score with one dart... Who can make it stick in the floor...

On an absolute scale there's just a single calibration so it's not much use, relativity is very funny and among beings with that perspective one guy stands apart specialising in coincidence, his name's not pronounceable in this type of space, a normal day for him is outside time, it's nothing to him, friends we couldn't imagine.

He's probably worse than anyone thinks but can't be absolutely hideous, friends only marginally less terrible, they must be pretty bad though someone probably loves them. Nice people often travel by bus, little grin for the conductor, smiles are currency, hello's an equivalent ten-bucks, coffee and a pastry yet nobody thinks to exploit it.

Here is there from a different perspective, geo-sequentially on and off a bus with a different point of view, time's not passing it's always new by quantum shifts, it probably shows-up in lots of dimensions. You could drop a bomb, they always do, take out the space and energy and there'll be nothing, no emptiness, only the past holding both the energy and space with an inconceivable negative bias in their state of existence.

I can fix this.. desire and faith may tip the scales but with nothing to throw or smash the emotional effort remains abstract inhibiting or maybe enhancing the function, a subjective point to the absolute reality we hope to influence, believing deeply in a subsequent change in the course of events and it works like nothing ever happened, I suppose it's good but can't say without a control subject.

Comfort and durability must be about a three, aesthetic about the same, three, empirical interface another three, enjoyment is low from the lame interface, an intoxicated two-point-four on general enjoyment, for a mean average less than three.. not a destination spot, it's a slum tour, the Entropy Cruise.. *My god, it's full of stars...* imagine the surprise, it looks like snowy random light, Where are we... This is nowhere... no-one says that, they don't know it's a place. Oh, this is just another dimension, good luck getting back out...

Shut-up Bill... Dammit Alice... they're behind in the rent on a smelly house in the depressed part of town, both lost their terrible job at the sludge-works and the truck's a wreck. Get the kids, we'll move into a cave... fresh air, plenty of dirt, running water whenever it rains, fall asleep huddled against an unknown threat and wake under a giant rock with trees outside. The kids love missing school and eagerly race to collect bush-food, watch the creek all day and don't spot a single yabby, Bill's holding a heavy stick checking under the shrubs for something to kill, Alice would sooner starve than dig for grubs, she reasons Fuck-off...

Pizza or burritos.. at the shop the guy's in conversation with a distraught record-producer, it seems someone's died, the guy nods in sympathy, Bill wants to help and enquires into the problem.. unless he plays drums he can piss-off. The boy drums, can count up to four... Well that's different... the studio's about half a mile down the street, they're tired and hungry and want pizza first.

Whatta'ya got, kid... the boy taps awkwardly at the equipment, a stick slips from his greasy fingers, he wipes his hands on his shirt and starts bashing at the drums in perfect time, Wow... The girl's in and out of jail and Bill strangles Alice. He's in the shadows panting and sweating looking nervously left and right, back against a wall, sirens fading into the night, he's not that far from his son's rock-star apartment.. the boy doesn't recognise him, hands someone a fifty for the homeless guy and has him shown out. The girl's on the stairs and drops the strap from her teeth to acknowledge dad, she jacks and shoots.. swoons.. he stands there like an idiot.

She opens her eyes, adjusts her jacket, Jesus dad, you look like shit... Yeah hi, you seem to be doin' alright, what's up... I was hoping to get something out of tight-arse... throws her purse at the door, Bill retrieves it and quietly slips the fifty inside, she'll always be his little girl, Fuck-off... so like her mother, she throws it back at the door, someone takes a look and shuts it again, she's storming out and seems to resent picking-up the purse, See ya'... Goodbye sweetheart... taking his place on the step, head in his hands, wishes he had some drugs.

22 Generic Parts

A girl in a shapeless khaki outfit stands focusing binoculars and remarks Birds are lovely this time of year… Hmm… the guy's marking time digesting the comment, this is all cold and bleak, sometimes snow right up to early spring when the birds return, he's seeing her in a new light, khakis, binoculars around her neck, a bum bag and hiking-boots, he comes-back with Yeah.. have you seen sheep in the snow… What about goats in a tree, something Dali put together, or Bosch... she has something in the binoculars, a wombat scratching around, times are hard.

Existence is suffering… he wasn't expecting that, barely knows her, reckons It could be worse, lucky they like grass… Bet they hate it, sick to death, grass again... Lemon grass must be nice, take your girlfriend there for dinner, I bet they'd go some molasses… Yes, they'd probably like some molasses… she's mumbling distantly peering through the lenses, Oh… a gasp bringing her hand up, ARGhh… drops the binoculars and turns away. He takes the glasses and looks over to see someone scrambling through the snow, it looks like a body down the bottom and blood spattered around, Shit, call someone… I've been trying, there's no signal… he watches the guy reach the top and climb into a green and white 4x4, can't make-out the number, focuses in time to catch the last three digits ..three-two-nine.. We'll probably get a signal up on the ridge… she's heading off through the cold but he knows a track and suggests back down to the left, it goes around to the top from the other side.

Did you get a good look at them… I only saw one scrambling up the bank, looked like some sort of gangster… Yeah, I thought so too.. they were just talking, one pulled out a knife and stabbed the other one right in the face…

An old lady slips into a room and quietly asks Are you alright, sweetheart... this guy's stripping-down a Triumph Speed-twin, a Tiger or a Bonnie, I don't know, the head's on the dresser but you can't tell, it could be a Trophy, there's valves on the bed in different states of polish, he sits on the edge, Hey Nan…

You used to be all speed-boats and scuba things, everything was always wet, but I suppose.. after your father… she trails-off picking-up his hand, Are you sure you're okay, love… he stares sorrowfully at the floor, she thinks he's still eight years old, that's nearly twenty years ago, he doesn't dive anymore, Thanks, Nan, I'm glad you're here… music starts somewhere, he finds the phone, Sorry Nanna, this is something, I might have to go… Alright love, go with your friends.. don't be too late, Mum's cooking dinner…

All he knows is the job's in two weeks, now they reckon it's tonight, he'll have to speak to Toni. No, you don't wanna bother Toni, who do you think gave the order.. just be there tonight and don't bring a piece… this is most irregular, his mind calls it bullshit, he has to show-up but won't just walk straight in, take a more discreet point of access, he'll be armed alright and just as well, there's a gang of strange guys sitting around cleaning and loading weapons, there's Doug but he doesn't see Toni, just those strangers. He gets a bead on the strangest one and picks him off with the silencer, then gets the guy next to him, bonus, WHAT'S THE STORY, DOUG… they look around but no-one spots him, he picks- off another two guys and moves quietly to the other end of the rafter, pop.. pop.. takes-out the last two, it's just him and Doug, he steps quickly in behind him bringing his hand around pressing a blade to his neck, Doug can't move, Wait a minute, let's talk this over… Talk what over, Doug, what is there to talk about… C'mon, you're a smart guy, all that money, think about it, it could be you an' me.. fifty-fifty down the line, what do you say… I'd say you're an idiot Doug, that's the dumbest thing I've ever heard… and drives the knife through his neck.

At his girlfriend's place Your grandmother called, she's worried about you… Yeah, she's very old… She's right, I worry sometimes too.. I know what you do, who you are and it scares me… That's too bad, sweetheart, I don't want to do this either… Then get-out, run, I'll go with you, they'll never find us… No, I don't want to do THIS.. takes her pretty face in his hands and twists her neck, success in any field takes sacrifice, sometimes throwing people under a bus, having them professionally thrown under and he's the guy you call, under busses, in front of trains, even over a cliff, it's all the same to him.

They're sitting down to breakfast when he finally gets home, he takes coffee and a piece of toast and stands by the sink, Hello dear, did you sleep well… Hey Nan, had a great night, how about you… I had to keep getting-up to check your grandfather, lucky he's alright… the old guy thinks it's funny. The TV's loud, kids getting cereal everywhere watching Transformers fight, he lowers the volume and the kids start eating again, robot-battle still raging, this must be a key episode, he catches a minute while they excitedly explain they're fighting over a thing that turns any machine into a Transformer.

Everyone's leaving the kitchen, just two cousins with old Frank and Nan at the table, he sits-in for some light conversation, You look great, first-day isn't it… Yep, start at ten… You excited… It's fuckin' K-Mart, I'll be on a register… That's just the tip of the iceberg, I love big retail it's a great job… Have you worked there… Target, in Queenbeyan, it's the same thing… Must have been nice… Yeah, lovely spot, a bit desperate but not far from the snow… You go skiing… Fuck-no, I got a job at the mall… Where was I all that time… Up on a sheep station I think, you were gone when I left… Oh yeah, cattle, that was fun but you get hurt, broken bones… You're from up north, eh Nanna,.. I'm from Longreach.. I met Frank on the station at Tenant Creek… Frank's from Sydney, he looks lost staring at the table and tells her Angel Arcade… What… he calls her Angel.. and touches her face, she doesn't know what to do and starts clearing plates.

What do you reckon, Frank… Yeah, I was going out to the shed, mate, work on me boxes… Boxes… Yeah, Canisters for a Minimalist Kitchen, for their own sake, you know minimalists… kisses Nanna pushing past in the doorway, our guy heads upstairs to get some sleep. It's dark when the phone wakes him up, Toni wants him, must be impressed with last nights handiwork.

WHAT the FUCK's going on.. Doug calls you and now he's dead with a bunch of guys from out-of-town, you double-crossing piece of shit…

No, wait, fellas, that's not.. BLAM.. At least he's not stupid anymore.. hey, that's the headstone... That's cold, Boss, someone has to tell his parents.. A boating accident... Why was he on a boat, he hated diving... Sorry, I meant an aeroplane accident, the propeller chopped him up bad, you don't want to see it... of course they want the body returned, the boys do some fast work on the corpse and retrieve the slug with a fire-axe.

That punk is a small part in the Toni story, there's no pictures no matter what you've heard, punks disappear every day, this is an empire dedicated to the smooth traverse of illicit goods and nobody cares about anyone or their grandmother. A lot of Nan's friends are dead, executed or traded across borders but there's still a strong network and they're glad to help. Satellites find Toni, pedestrians brush past planting surveillance equipment, if this guy sneezes we'll know about it, grab him when he's over his cold. He has a bag over his head, hands bound, blood and sweat stain his t-shirt, it's probably him, why would they lie, Here he is, Granny... Thanks... she presses a .38 to the bag, fires one shot and kicks the body from the helicopter, she did it to her son-in-law nearly twenty years ago, told her grandson his father disappeared skin-diving and swore then she'd make it up to him. Tears are forming in her eyes gazing out the open chopper, This one's for you, sweetheart...

23 I love this... Desire it... What... Nuthin', what was it... This, I love coming to this pub, who's havin' a Boiler-maker... Just a beer, thanks... Ah-huh, you want one... Yeah, Boiler-maker sounds good, what is it... the start of an epic night. Three schooners and two shots of whisky, thanks... the attractive girl gets the drinks back to the table with barely an ogling, it's early, a few hours later the girls are stumbling loudly along the footpath into an Uber to someone's place for music and drugs, It's real, it's just not us... What... Who is it... Yeah, it's us, and it's real, but it's not our reality... Fuck off... You know what I mean... Lobsang Rampa, A Separate Reality. you reading that... No, what, I was just thinking there's all this time... No, don't... Eh, what about time...

That's how they meet, not long after that the first kid arrives by I.V.F, and a mortgage, struggle with the rat-race, kids coming thick and fast, adoptions and surrogates, a second mortgage and no longer above breaking the law arrested the first time, something minor, fake cards. Suspended sentence and straight back into the crimes on an international level laundering money through art galleries.

The women are not only smart they're also lovely, nobody notices the ridiculous over-head, every kid needs an off-shore account, attractive real-estate, tax deductible house full of Au-pair and tutors while the mothers indulge at quiet places on the Mediterranean, Thank-you Renoir… the art never moves, it's just cyphers and crypto transfers across borders at specific times and favourable rates, an AI doing the communication and everyone takes a cut. They're rubbing shoulders with people that aren't there, they never go out, rub each others shoulders even after all these years. It's a shame when they break each others heart, destroy each other with insults, their friends are in tears Ask her, she did it first… You did, you skanky old ho... Fuck off… something's changed, it's the future and everybody wins.

Nothing or something it doesn't matter, wattage is what counts, and with limited resource there's nothing that might constitute profit, no dividend from outside reality, there's only work. No beginning or end, always right in the middle, funny but also tragic and a bit sexy congealed from homogeneous space, a clot of individuals struggling doing a lot of work.

What's mine is mine… the logic's good, by definition it's theirs, tragic and funny and I think the ladies like the brutality, I don't know, women are so mysterious, they might imagine themselves with a share of whatever the moron claims to possess.

Drowning or on fire wouldn't matter, a chemical state, entropy so complex it probably won't survive, the tip of a dynamic iceberg with treacherous sunsets, poignant wars and love constantly on every planet in every species, a mess of pheromones, spores, viruses and bacteria.. the smell.

There's a wake for the punk, his corpse stretched out in a closed casket. The gang put his bike back together and wheel it into the lounge for the party and they start pushing each other through the house while quiet conversation swings around to his father's disappearance now him so young. They look again at the kids grabbing cakes and hiding under the tables, wonder which will die first, who's got the gene, CRASH… idiots, barely room for them to turn the bike in the lounge, everyone's backed into a corner or squeezed into the middle spilling as little alcohol as possible.

Conversation resumes trying to vocalise an experience, compromising, finding a common denominator more brutal and ignorant than you'd expect, mostly all third-party all drunker than each other confident we're laughing at some other stupid bastards. That's not really how it goes, it's more lies and brutal control, these bastards stick together like Lego blocks in a sub-set of a big mosaic picture that dwarfs this one and consumes every other picture laughing nostalgically, Aliens took our planet…it's the punchline for a lot of jokes in an elegant higher plane with serenity floating on turmoil, screams and moans forming a dense stable atmosphere, sharing the hope for a happy ending knowing it's a vicious lie.

9 781923 609440